Airplanes and Other Things That Fly

By Steve Kelley
Illustrated by Tom LaPadula

A GOLDEN BOOK • NEW YORK
Western Publishing Company, Inc., Racine, Wisconsin 53404

Long, long ago, people watched the birds in the sky and dreamed about flying. If birds could fly, why not people?

There are many stories from all over the world about people flying in ancient times. A Persian king was said to have flown by making four eagles carry his throne. In Greece, Daedalus was supposed to have made wings of feathers and wax for himself and his son.

No one thinks these things really happened. They are stories that show man's curiosity about being airborne. As centuries passed this curiosity continued. The Chinese invented the first simple flying machines: kites and skyrockets. Centuries later the great inventor Leonardo Da Vinci designed several flying machines that could carry people, but he never built them.

In France in 1783, two brothers, the Montgolfiers, built their idea of a flying machine. They had noticed that smoke or hot air always travels upward. They made a giant balloon and used a firepot to heat the air beneath it. As the air warmed it pushed the balloon up into the sky. One day they rode in the balloon for five miles. After dreaming about it for centuries, human beings were flying!

Balloons, however, could only go where the wind blew them. Inventors still dreamed of being able to fly wherever they wanted to go, like birds. They built all sorts of flying machines with motors. Most of these machines would flap, rotate, flutter, and do everything *but* fly.

At Kitty Hawk, North Carolina, in 1903, two other brothers, the Wrights, built an airplane based on early gliders. But this plane, the Wright Flyer, had its own motor and a propeller. The plane took off and...flew! The flight was only twelve seconds long, but that was long enough to change the skies forever.

Sopwith
Camel

Spad

Fokker
Triplane

12

Fokker Triplane

Curtiss Jenny

More and more airplanes with propellers were built. Flights became longer and longer. Only a little more than ten years after that first peaceful flight, airplanes were used as weapons of war. In World War I, fast little planes fired their machine guns as they fought for control of the skies. Most of these warplanes were biplanes, like the British Sopwith Camel. Germany's greatest pilot, the Red Baron, flew a red Fokker Triplane, which had three wings.

In the golden age of airplanes that followed World War I, pilots were heroes. Charles Lindbergh made a daring long-distance flight to show the world what airplanes could do. Alone in his tiny plane, the *Spirit of St. Louis,* he made the first flight from New York to Paris across a stormy Atlantic Ocean.

Other pilots found fame and thrills in racing. Jimmy Doolittle flew the stubby *Gee Bee* racer to victory in the Thompson Trophy races while a crowd of thousands watched.

With all airplanes could do, they still weren't strong enough to carry passengers across the oceans. This job was left to dirigibles, giant balloons with motors. A dirigible was like a flying ocean liner, with a dining room, kitchen, and bedrooms. It took the *Graf Zeppelin* four days to carry 60 passengers from Germany to the United States.

Ford Trimotor

Boeing Clipper

NX 78107

PAN AMERICAN AM

18

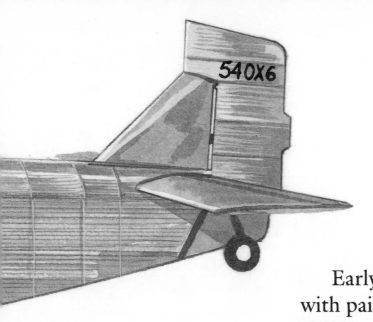

Early airplanes had been made of wood frames covered with painted cloth. The Ford Trimotor was the first airliner made completely out of metal. It was nicknamed the "Tin Goose." The Trimotor had three motors and could hold eight passengers.

The first airliner able to cross the ocean was a big seaplane. Seaplanes, like the Boeing Clipper, could land on the water in an emergency. This seaplane was so big that its crew could walk around inside the wings and work on the engines during a flight!

Unlike the big, heavy seaplanes, the Piper Cub was small and light. It often served as a training plane for pilots. To start a Piper Cub a person had to spin the propeller by hand. The plane had no starter motor or battery. Many Piper Cubs are still being flown today.

The cropduster is another small propeller plane. A cropduster sprays crops to protect them from bugs. In just a few minutes, one of these planes can spray a field that would take hours to spray from the ground.

New and different passenger planes continued to be built. One of the most popular passenger planes of all times was the DC-3, which was sleek, fast, and quiet when compared to the planes that had come before it. However, DC-3's did more than just carry passengers. During World War II, they dropped paratroopers into enemy territory and carried heavy cargo all over the world.

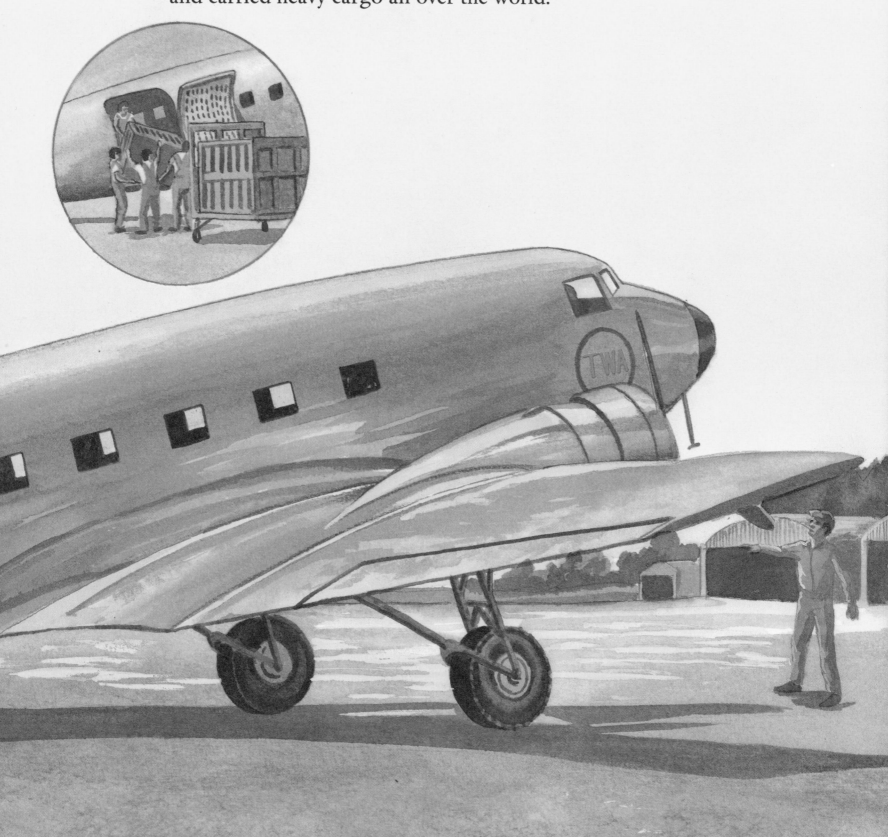

Spitfire

238091

B-17 Bomber

Airplanes played an even bigger role in the battles of World War II than they had in World War I. The DC-3 was just one of many planes that soared among the clouds, fighting for control of the skies. Enemy planes chased and fired at one another, while bombers let loose their weapons on those below.

Messerschmitt ME-109

One of the most famous fighter planes was the German Messerschmitt ME-109, at one time the fastest fighter plane in the world. The British Supermarine Spitfire proved to be a worthy opponent of the ME-109. America's Boeing B-17 Flying Fortress Bomber was another able-bodied aircraft during the war. It carried nearly six tons of bombs and had more than ten machine guns!

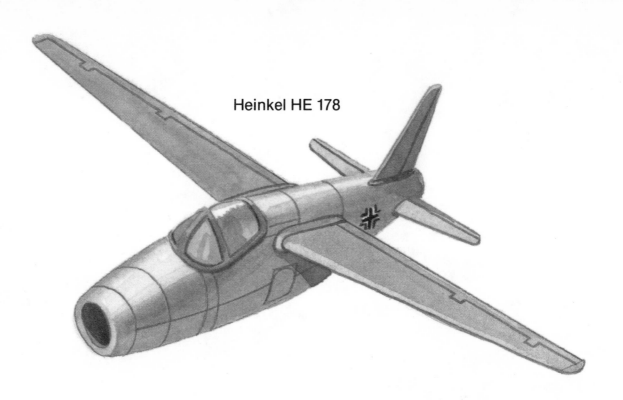

Heinkel HE 178

Toward the end of World War II a new type of airplane appeared. It had a different kind of engine and no propellers. The new engine was called a jet engine. Planes with jet engines became known as jets. Yet one more time aircraft and air travel underwent a major change. Jets could go much faster than propeller planes. The German-built Heinkel HE 178 was the first jet plane. The British De Havilland Comet was the first jet passenger plane.

De Havilland Comet

Boeing 707

In America the Boeing 707 was the first successful jet passenger plane. The biggest jet passenger plane is the Boeing 747, which can carry 500 people.

Boeing 747

Today airplanes travel very fast. They can even fly faster than the speed of sound. The first airplane to break the sound barrier was a Bell X-1 plane, flown by Chuck Yeager, an Air Force test pilot. The Concorde SST is a passenger plane that can fly at *twice* the speed of sound! The Concorde can fly from New York to England in just three and a half hours.

A helicopter has a rotor blade at its top. This rotor blade allows the helicopter to fly straight up or down, sideways, backward, or even to hover in one spot.

Helicopters can land in more places than airplanes, since helicopters do not need runways. Because of this, the helicopter has a variety of special uses. A helicopter can carry passengers or be a flying ambulance. Other helicopters are used by the Coast Guard, the military, and the police. Still other helicopters are used to help report about traffic for local news stations.

The most famous name in helicopters is Igor Sikorsky. Sikorsky designed the first successful helicopter that had a single rotor in 1939. Later Sikorsky models included strong helicopters that could lift heavy equipment, including pipes and even trucks!

There are some places where the best aircraft to have is neither a helicopter nor a standard airplane. In the far north of Alaska, for example, where there are more lakes and rivers than airports, the best aircraft is a floatplane. In the warm months, floats on the plane allow it to land right on the water. In the winter, skis let the plane land on the frozen water.

Although most aircraft are designed to be useful machines, some airplanes are built mainly for fun. Aerobatic planes are built to do tricks in the air. These planes fly in contests and air shows, thrilling the crowds below with their fancy flying. They can swoop up and down and even roll over and over.

As far as air travel has come since those very long-ago days of watching birds fly, people still like to glide through the air, either on gliders or in sailplanes. Some gliders look like airplanes but they have no motors. Others are hang gliders, with big wings and bars.

The *Gossamer Condor* is very much like a flying bicycle. It has no motor but is instead powered by pedals. The pilot pedals away beneath huge wings.

There are a lot of modern defense aircraft. These include the F-14 Tomcat, the Navy's topgun fighter jet. The F-14 shoots into the air from the deck of an aircraft-carrier ship.

Hawker Harrier

The Hawker Harrier is a British-designed defense aircraft. The Harrier can take off and land vertically. This means it can hide well from an enemy, since it does not need a large airfield, something that is easy for an enemy to spot.

Most airplanes are tracked from the ground by radar and appear on radar screens. However, the United States Stealth Bomber can fly undetected by radar due to a variety of features, including its winglike shape.

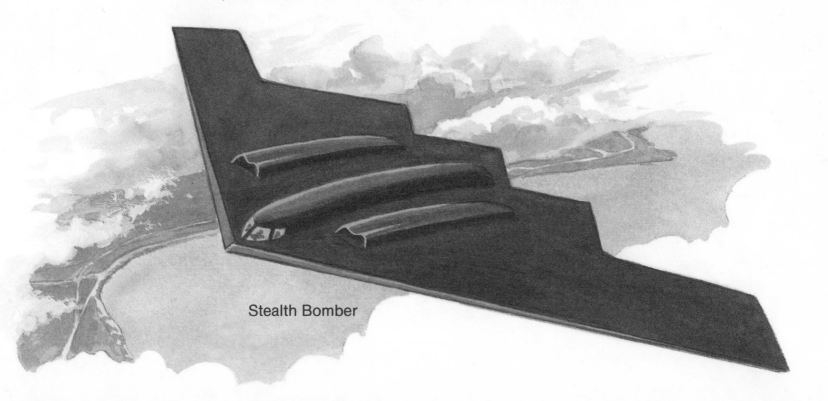

Stealth Bomber

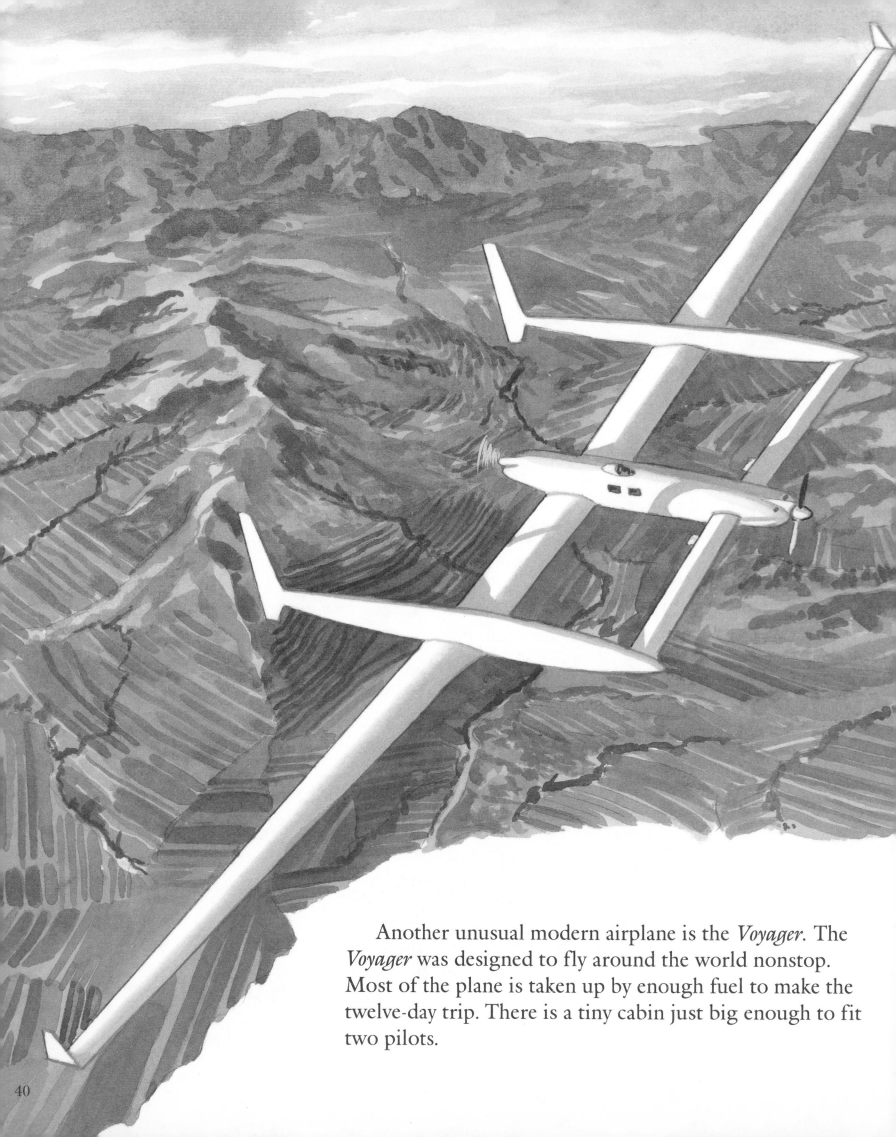

Another unusual modern airplane is the *Voyager*. The *Voyager* was designed to fly around the world nonstop. Most of the plane is taken up by enough fuel to make the twelve-day trip. There is a tiny cabin just big enough to fit two pilots.

Flying machines can now do many amazing things. They can even go into deep space, the dark part of the universe, where there is no air or gravity. The Russians were the first to send a man into space, but the United States quickly followed. Alan Shepard was the first United States astronaut to go into space. He flew in the Redstone Rocket in 1961.

UNITED STATES

The United States space program continued to build rockets and send men into space. The goal was to land a man on the Moon. The 363-foot-high Saturn V rocket was the first rocket engine that took astronauts to the Moon. Inside the huge rocket were three fuel tanks. An Apollo spacecraft sat on top of the tanks. The spacecraft contained a command, a service, and a lunar module.

One by one the tanks ran out of fuel and, having done their job of boosting the whole machine up, they broke off and fell away. While one astronaut waited in the command module, two other astronauts took the lunar module and touched down on the Moon in 1969.

Space travel has continued to progress since that breathtaking day when Neil Armstrong became the first man ever to set foot on the Moon. The Space Shuttle is the first space vehicle that can actually fly deep into space and return to Earth so that it may be used again. With its 78-foot wingspan, the Space Shuttle looks a little like a regular airplane, but it needs to take off attached to a huge rocket.

UNITED STATES OF AMERICA

While all manned spacecraft go into space and return, there are hundreds of flying machines called satellites that are launched into space and stay there. Satellites do many helpful jobs. Some help predict the weather. Others are used to study the conditions in space. Still others send television programs or telephone calls from one place to another.

Flying machines have traveled an enormous distance from that very first hot-air balloon ride taken by the Montgolfier brothers. If people continue to dream of flying, there will be no limit to the types of aircraft we may see. As long as mankind's imagination soars, so will flying machines!